To Robin Smith.

Library of Congress Cataloging-in-Publication Data available.

ISBN 978-1-4521-5288-2

Manufactured in China.

Design by Sara Gillingham Studio.
Handlettering by Sergio Ruzzier.
The illustrations in this book were rendered in pen, ink, and watercolor.

10 9 8 7 6 5 4 3 2 1

Chronicle Books LLC
680 Second Street
San Francisco, California 94107
www.chroniclekids.com

GIO RUZZIER'S

X + CHICK

THE PARTY

and Other Stories

chronicle books · san francisco

CONTENTS

THE PARTY

I am reading this book.

How can you be reading that book if you are talking to me?

You are right, Chick. I WAS reading this book. And I will go back to reading right now.

SLAM!

TICK
TOCK

TICK
TOCK

9

TICK
TOCK

Chick, are you okay?

CRASH!

THUD!

SPLASH!

Chick, I am coming in!

11

14

GOOD SOUP

Fox, foxes are supposed to eat field mice, not carrots!

I don't like to eat field mice.

Fox, foxes are supposed to eat frogs, not onions!

I don't like to
eat frogs.

Fox, foxes are
supposed to eat moles,
not potatoes!

Foxes are supposed to eat chipmunks.

And they're supposed to eat squirrels . . .

lizards . . .

and little birds.

Little birds?

Yes, Fox,
little bir...

Uh-oh.

26

SIT STILL

This is a good spot.

I will paint a nice landscape.

What are you doing, Fox?

I'm painting a landscape.

No problem. I can sit still for as long as you want.

This rock is not very soft.

Of course it's not very soft. It is a rock.

I will go and get a pillow. Then I will sit still on that rock.

Fox, you can paint my portrait now.

Just sit still, please.

I am hungry.

You just ate three bowls of soup.

I will go and get a snack. Then I will sit very still on that rock.

CRUNCH

How's that portrait coming?

Just sit very still, please.

I am thirsty.

Of course you are thirsty. You ate a whole bag of potato chips.

I will go and get a drink. Then I will sit very, very still on that rock.

SLURP

Fox, you can finish
my portrait now.

I am done with
my painting.

You are
done
with my
portrait?!

I could not paint your
portrait because
you did not sit still.

You are a good painter, Fox.

Thank you, Chick.

You should paint a portrait of me one day.